Yellowbelly and Plum Go to School

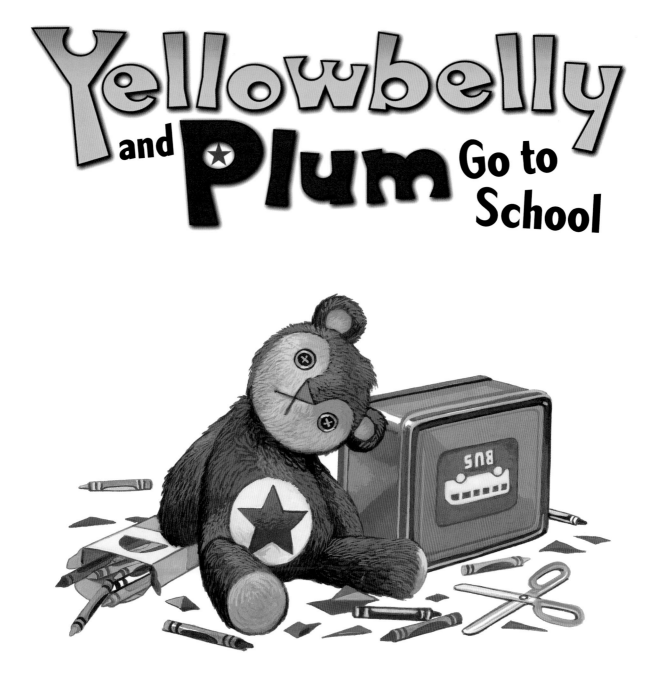

Nathan Hale

G. P. Putnam's Sons

For my Mom and Dad

G. P. PUTNAM'S SONS

A division of Penguin Young Readers Group.

Published by The Penguin Group.

Penguin Group (USA) Inc., 375 Hudson Street, New York, NY 10014, U.S.A.

Penguin Group (Canada), 90 Eglinton Avenue East, Suite 700, Toronto, Ontario, Canada M4P 2Y3

(a division of Pearson Penguin Canada Inc.).

Penguin Books Ltd, 80 Strand, London WC2R 0RL, England.

Penguin Ireland, 25 St. Stephen's Green, Dublin 2, Ireland (a division of Penguin Books Ltd.).

Penguin Group (Australia), 250 Camberwell Road, Camberwell, Victoria 3124, Australia (a division of Pearson Australia Group Pty Ltd).

Penguin Books India Pvt Ltd, 11 Community Centre, Panchsheel Park, New Delhi - 110 017, India.

Penguin Group (NZ), Cnr Airborne and Rosedale Roads, Albany, Auckland 1310, New Zealand (a division of Pearson New Zealand Ltd).

Penguin Books (South Africa) (Pty) Ltd, 24 Sturdee Avenue, Rosebank, Johannesburg 2196, South Africa.

Penguin Books Ltd, Registered Offices: 80 Strand, London WC2R 0RL, England.

Published simultaneously in Canada. Manufactured in China by South China Printing Co. Ltd.

Design by Katrina Damkoehler. Text set in Tema Cantante Sans.

The artist used Golden Acrylics on illustration board to create the illustrations for this book.

Library of Congress Cataloging-in-Publication Data

Hale, Nathan, 1976–

Yellowbelly and Plum go to school / Nathan Hale.   p. cm.

Summary: On his first day of school, Yellowbelly brings along his best friend Plum, a stuffed bear,

but when Plum goes missing, Yellowbelly discovers that they both have made a lot of new friends.

[1. Teddy bears—Fiction. 2. First day of school—Fiction.] 1. Title.

PZ7.H13757Yel 2007   [E]—dc22   2006026296

ISBN 978-0-399-24624-1

1 3 5 7 9 10 8 6 4 2

First Impression

Yellowbelly and Plum were best pals.

They did everything together.

envelope

and orthodontist.

When Yellowbelly started school, Plum went with him.

They thought school would be
a very fun game to play.

Yellowbelly said
"Hallo!"
to all the kids, but Plum was shy.
So Yellowbelly introduced him.

"He's Plum!"

Yellowbelly got his own desk and so did Plum.

At music time,
Yellowbelly played the glockenspiel,

and Plum played drums.

During art class,
Yellowbelly made
a finger painting.

Plum made
a bear painting.

Plum was an excellent student

ORCHARD ELEMENTARY

BRIGHT
YOUNG
THINGS

and so was Yellowbelly.

Recess was outside.
Yellowbelly climbed the jungle gym
to help save the day.

While he was up there,
Plum met a new friend.

When Yellowbelly came back down, Plum was gone.
"Where, oh, where is Plum?"
he said.

Plum was playing basketball.

"Poor Plum! He's lost!"
Yellowbelly started to cry.

Plum wasn't lost; he was busy playing Frisbee

and dogcatcher.

He was not shy anymore.

Yellowbelly cried louder and louder.
"Don't be sad," said a little girl.

But Yellowbelly couldn't help it.

"I miss Plum so bad!"

he cried.

"Plum's playing over there," said the little girl.
"He's so fun."
Yellowbelly looked and saw—

"plum!"

He ran and hugged his friend.

"I missed you, Plum."

Plum missed Yellowbelly too.

Plum showed Yellowbelly
how to play basketball.

Then Plum and Yellowbelly taught everybody
how to play envelope,

meteor shower,

and orthodontist.

OCT 2007

H
A   Hale, Nathan

Yellowbelly and Plum
Go to School.

$16.99